GW00865876

GW00865876

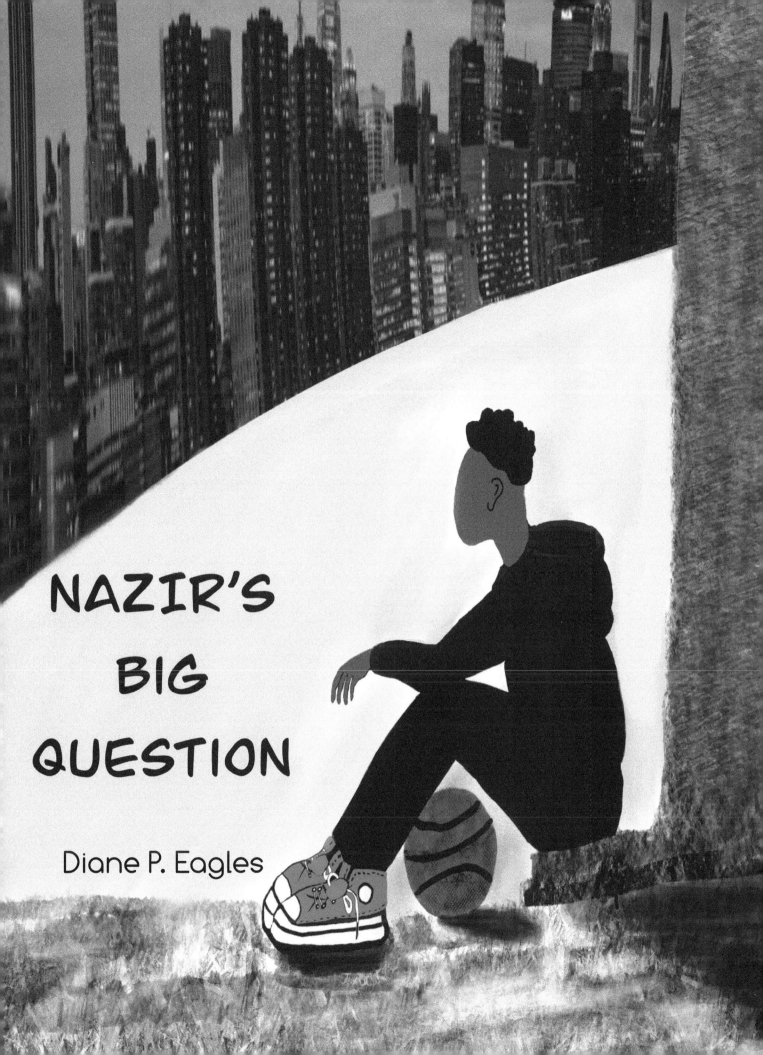

NAZIR'S
BIG
QUESTION

Diane P. Eagles

Copyright © 2021 Diane P. Eagles.

All rights reserved. No part of this book may be used or reproduced by any means, graphic, electronic, or mechanical, including photocopying, recording, taping or by any information storage retrieval system without the written permission of the author except in the case of brief quotations embodied in critical articles and reviews.

This is a work of fiction. All of the characters, names, incidents, organizations, and dialogue in this novel are either the products of the author's imagination or are used fictitiously.

WestBow Press books may be ordered through booksellers or by contacting:

WestBow Press
A Division of Thomas Nelson & Zondervan
1663 Liberty Drive
Bloomington, IN 47403
www.westbowpress.com
844-714-3454

Because of the dynamic nature of the Internet, any web addresses or links contained in this book may have changed since publication and may no longer be valid. The views expressed in this work are solely those of the author and do not necessarily reflect the views of the publisher, and the publisher hereby disclaims any responsibility for them.

Any people depicted in stock imagery provided by Getty Images are models, and such images are being used for illustrative purposes only.
Certain stock imagery © Getty Images.

Front cover photo by Karen Myers Frank

Interior Image Credit: Diane P. Eagles

Scripture quotations are from the ESV® Bible (The Holy Bible, English Standard Version®), copyright © 2001 by Crossway, a publishing ministry of Good News Publishers. Used by permission. All rights reserved.

ISBN: 978-1-6642-3333-1 (sc)
ISBN: 978-1-6642-3332-4 (hc)
ISBN: 978-1-6642-3334-8 (e)

Library of Congress Control Number: 2021909214

Print information available on the last page.

WestBow Press rev. date: 8/5/2021

Behold, children are a heritage from the Lord, the fruit of the womb a reward.

Psalm 127:3

A Note to Grown-Ups

Anxiety and depression, and other mental health issues are becoming more common in young children and teenagers. Recognizing the early signs and symptoms are crucial. If your child is exhibiting any of the following characteristics, consult your child's physician or other health care providers. Ask for advice and seek resources to help your child work through their anxiety and depression.

Throughout *Nazir's Big Question*, there are examples of a child exhibiting a few mental health symptoms mentioned below.

If you notice that these feelings are persistent and lasting longer than normal, this may signify depression or other mental health issues.

- Children may feel sad, hopeless, or even irritable.

- Feeling worthless, useless, or guilty is another sign of depression.

- If you notice any changes in eating patterns — eating more or less than usual — this could also signify that your child may be struggling with depression.

- Headaches are a common symptom of depression.

- Changes in sleep patterns — sleeping more or less than usual.

If your child shows self-injury or destructive behavior, seek professional help *immediately*. This more severe sign of depression can lead to life-threatening situations.

Today was one of those days. A head full of thoughts and nowhere to rest them.

Tired from a sleepless night, Nazir slowly dragged himself to the breakfast table. The warm morning sun was brightly shining, but it just as well been dark and cold. Nazir's favorite breakfast smelled delicious, but it had no taste as he poked it in his mouth.

Nothing was normal, or the way things used to be, that is. Most of Nazir's 7th-grade class was barely showing up for school on Zoom. They sometimes came wearing pajamas, doo rags, or rollers in their hair. And entering stores was strange, everyone wore a mask. In the place of cell phones, they now carried a small bottle of sanitizer in their hands.

The COVID-19 virus is everywhere and people are dying. Nazir's mom works the midnight shift at the hospital as a nurse. She is always tired and cries a lot. She said her job as a nurse was hard. Nazir thinks about his mom and grandmother becoming sick or dying. It frightens him.

THAT VIRUS IS SCARY!

Nazir thought about last year this time, his birthday. He got sad thinking about no party and no getting together with friends. He wanted to be with his friends at school and church. He missed them. To his surprise, he even missed some of his teachers.

As basketball team captain, winning the State Championship for Nazir was everything. He and his best friend Kasaun were to play Grade State Championships this year. But with Covid, there were no plans of moving forward. No practice or schedule of returning for games. He heard that two of his coaches Brown and Jones, are quarantined.

And then, there were the angry crowds of people. As cameras scanned the masses, waves of people slowly walked, screamed, and yelled for miles and miles. They marched with open mouths and signs that read "Black Lives Matter," "Say Their Names," and "No Justice, No Peace."

On the internet, Nazir saw people killed by police. He wondered, could that happen to him?

One day a storekeeper called the police because he thought Nazir had stolen something. Nazir tried to tell the angry man that he stole nothing. He was sweating, but he shivered and felt cold. He cried and wanted to go home.

The storekeeper held him in a back room. The police arrived and searched Nazir's whole body, head to toe, but found nothing.

Nazir's heart beats faster when he thinks about that day.

But Nazir had a bigger problem.

His thoughts took up most of his days and nights, making him feel sick. Sometimes he had nightmares. He was terrified.

The moon cast strange shadows on the walls. There's a Percheron he imagined, tall, clean-limbed, and powerful with its beautiful red tassels and a shiny silver harness. He remembered seeing one at the North America Draft Horse Show last year. As he thought less of his cares and troubles and more on the magnificent horse, he slowly drifted to sleep.

Nazir wanted to tell someone about all the things that troubled him and made him sad. So, the next morning Nazir decided to turn to the smartest person he knew, his grandma, Big Ma Nona. She had come to live with Nazir, his two little brothers Tre' von and Syair, and his mom. The house was always buzzing with engaging conversations and filled with delicious food.

Big Ma traveled all over the world as an environmental scientist. She knew a lot. And when she did not have the answers, she always knew where to begin to find them. Her books were about cool people, exotic places, and peculiar things. Some of her books could make you laugh or cry, while others just made you mad.

One day Nazir grabbed one of Big Ma's books from her shelf. The book was *We've Got a Job: The 1963 Birmingham Children's March* by Jane Addams. He was very surprised when Big Ma proudly said, "I was there." Her Sunday school class marched with Dr. Martin Luther King Jr. in Birmingham, Alabama. She was only 12 years old.

The people marched and boycotted businesses because they were treated badly and disrespected through unfair voting and segregation laws in the south."

Later that year, four little girls from her Sunday School class were killed in a church bombing. Her life changed that day. In her heart, she learned to trust and believe that God would always faithfully lead and protect her, even when she was sad and afraid. Nazir thought his Big Ma Nona was the coolest. A radical history changer. He hoped that one day he, too, could do something to make the lives of other people better.

After schoolwork, Nazir headed to find Big Ma.

The aroma of a warm lemon pound cake and the gentle rattle of pots and pans led Nazir on a trail to the kitchen. Big Ma was busy getting dinner ready. Sitting down a little harder than he intended, Nazir startled Big Ma. She looked up over her glasses and ask "How are you doing today, Nazir?"

Taking a deep breath, Nazir began talking. He talked about how he was afraid of the virus, afraid of the family becoming sick or dying, the killings of unarmed Black men, and how he missed his friends. Nazir told Big Ma all the things that were troubling him and making him sad. Big Ma nodded her head as she quietly listened.

Finally, Nazir asked, "Big Ma, why does my life matter? Big Ma Nona looked at Nazir with a smile as if she was about to give him a special

present and said, "Nazir, I would like to read something to you."

Then, she wiped her hands on the kitchen towel and reached for her Bible on top of the shelf. She joined Nazir at the table, opened her Bible, and read the creation story in Genesis.

"In the beginning God created the heavens and earth" she said.

Big Ma continued, "On the first day, He created light. On the second day, He created the sky.

And on the third — He created the land, seas, and all kinds of plants and trees.

And on the fourth day, God created the sun, moon, and stars to give us signs and seasons.

On the fifth day, God created the birds of the air and the sea's fish. And after each day, God saw all that He had made and said it was good.

On the last day of creating — the sixth day — He made all the living creatures and creeping things."

Nazir squirmed in his chair and thought maybe Big Ma had forgotten his question. So, he asked again "But Big Ma, what about me? What does God say about me? What makes "me" being "me" so special?"

"Well, Nazir, you see God saved His most precious creation until that last day. He made all these things — the sun and moon and animals and trees — so that His most wonderful and precious creation, **YOU**, had a beautiful place in which to enjoy Him and live. When you were in your mama's belly," she said with a chuckle, "God knew you. He made you on purpose for a purpose." God's purpose for us began at the beginning of life.

Big Ma continued to read.

"So, God created mankind in His own image, in the image of God he created them; male and female."

And on the seventh day, after God saw everything that He had made, He said, "It is very good." And He rested.

" Nazir, every man, woman, boy and girl, since the first, Adam and Eve, are made in God's image. People are different from all other living creatures for a reason. God created us to **know Him**, and He wants to **know us**. We were all made, special, each one of us, on purpose," Big Ma said. She continued "We belong to a holy, loving, powerful, and just God, and He wants you to know that Nazir. You may not realize what your purpose is yet, but as you continue to grow in strength and knowledge, you will gain confidence in your abilities."

Then Big Ma threw her head back and laughed and said, "but God has a way of using things we didn't even know about ourselves for His plan and glory. He uses children's lives just as He may use an adult's life. In 1963, our voices and nonviolent actions as children resulted in talks and agreements that changed laws. As a result, the lunch counters in public places, businesses, and restrooms became available. Now, people could sit where they wanted, and hiring opportunities for Black people improved.

Big Ma smiled and asked, "Remember when I said that God is a just God?"

Nazir nodded his head yes. She continued, "that means God's ways are always fair and right. He wants us to act right and fair and to do what is good and right for ourselves and others."

Nazir thought about his basketball coaches and referees and how God was different from them. They were not always fair or right.

Placing her Bible back on the shelf, she turned to stir the hot boiling pot of green beans. Big Ma said, "there is something deep down in each of us that makes every human worthy of **respect** and **dignity**."

Nazir asked, "how will I know when I have not treated someone with dignity? What if I forget and get it wrong?" Patting butter on the biscuits, Big Ma chuckled and said, "Well, sometimes it's not easy to know, but here are some things to keep in mind. Try to show respect for other people's bodies, life, and voice no matter how small or different from your own, even when you disagree.

Feeling embarrassed, Nazir swallowed hard and held his head down. He remembered when he had acted wrong towards others by fighting, calling them names, and having mean and evil thoughts about them.

As if Big Ma knew what Nazir was thinking, she continued and said, "we all get it wrong, Nazir, but always be willing to say you are sorry, to God first, then to the one you hurt.

Would you like to be called out of your name? Or for people to hurt or harm you?" Nazir had never thought about it that way before. He was only aware of his feelings and how other's insults hurt him. No, he didn't like to be called names, harmed, or treated badly.

Big Ma said, "God wants us to pray, talk to Him and ask for His help. Nazir, I learned to pray as a young girl growing up in Alabama. I saw and heard many terrible things I didn't understand. I realized that I could not control sickness, death, or natural disasters, like tornadoes and earthquakes. These things sometimes make us afraid or sad. Life has many hardships and uncertainties. Hope is always there. We must find that hope to move us forward.

Big Ma said she had many questions too as a young person. By asking those questions made her the person, she is today. "Highly favored and blessed by God," Big Ma Nona said with a wide grin. Then Big Ma hung up her apron, turned off the hot stove, and grabbed a stack of bowls, in one big swoop, as only Big Ma Nona could do.

"Now Nazir," said Big Ma," let's get that table set, and then you go and call your brothers down for dinner." Nazir could not wait for dinner! He was starving! Big Ma moved down the hall quickly, with arms weighed down with delicious food. Nazir, carrying a bundle of forks and knives, could hear Big Ma's voice trail off. She asked, "Nazir Did I ever tell you about the time I traveled to South Africa? I meet Nelson Mandela during his 1991 presidential inauguration.

Nazir knew that he and his brother were in store for another one of Big Ma's exciting adventures.

A Note to Kids

Nazir still had many questions about things he did not understand and made him afraid. He felt better knowing that **a loving God created him on purpose for a purpose** and good things were possible for his life. Big Ma was there to listen to him. He learned how important it is to talk about how you feel inside, even when it is difficult, and you are afraid and sad. Nazir realized that he is responsible for the thoughts in his head. Your thinking can change from bad and negative to good and positive, about yourself or other people. And he had more control over his thoughts than he realized. Even as a kid, it is important to understand what you think and feel and why you feel the way you do. It's okay to ask for help. Sometimes talking about your thoughts and feelings is just what's needed. Nazir was happy to know that God's thoughts about him are good and **God is all-powerful**. He cares about children's fears, pain, and disappointments.

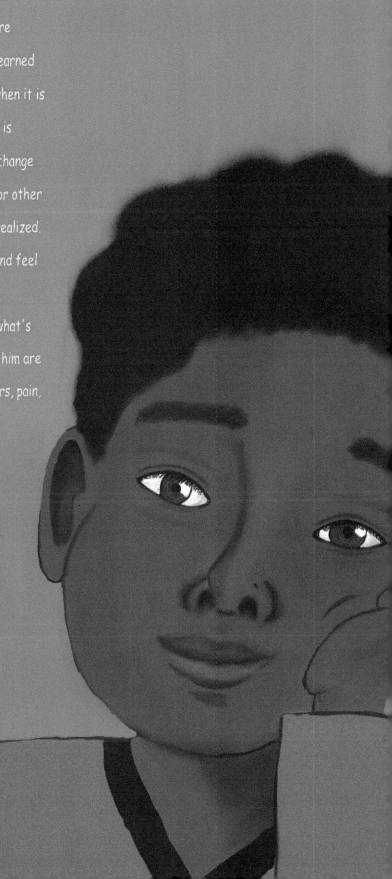

My birthday was not as bad as I thought it would be. I met up with a few of my friends on the internet to play video games. Later that day, some parents had a neighborhood scavenger hunt with delicious food at each station. My mom made sure that we were all being Covid safe. I started keeping a journal, to remind me to be thankful and one day, I'm going to write a book and let people know what it was like to live through a global pandemic.

Oh Yeah, Check out my GOAT (greatest of all times) Self-Care page. It's cool and helps me out a lot. When I feel stressed out or over things, I look at this page, pick something to do, and go chill. Hey, make one up for yourself; I'm adding on to mine all the time as I discover ways to take care of myself. Feel free to use some of the things that help me.

SELF-CARE

BUILDING BLOCKS TO A HEALTHY ME !

BE TIME

WISE

EAT HEALTHY FOODS

REST/SLEEP   **STAY CONNECTED**

BE ACTIVE

Hey, did you know that no two people share the same fingerprints?

God loves you!

He created you as a one-of-a-kind. There is no one else who looks, thinks, or does things quite like you. **You are special** and made for a unique purpose. Really! God's plans for you are good (Jer. 29:11). He wants you to know Him through a relationship with Him. No matter who you are and what you have done. God's **love** and acceptance of you are greater than any **sin** (things that we say, do, or think that displeases God).

We have **all sinned** (Rom. 3:23). **God is holy** (perfect), and our sin keeps us from having a relationship with Him. Because of **God's love** (Jn. 3:16), He had a plan to send Jesus to die for sin. **Jesus willingly** (He didn't put up a fight) took our punishment for sin so we could receive forgiveness (Rom. 5:8). Jesus died, was buried, and on the third day, He arose from the dead (1 Cor. 15: 3-4).

God wants you to live with Him **now and forever!**

That's GOOD NEWS!

Are you ready to have your sins forgiven and start your new life with Jesus? You can begin right now with this prayer.

Dear God, I know I have done wrong things. I have sinned, and I am sorry.
I believe Your Son Jesus died for me and came back to life after three days.
All because you love me. Please help me. I need You. Thank you for making me Your child!
In Jesus' name,
Amen!

" My steadfast love shall not depart from you." Isaiah 54:10
"The Lord (God) is *my helper*; I will not fear." Hebrews 13:6
" The Lord *is near* to all who call on Him." Psalm 145:18
" See what kind of *love* the Father has given to us, that we should be called children of God!"
1 John 3:1

AUTHOR'S NOTE

Many people grew up hearing the phrase, "children should be seen and not heard." This old English proverbial phrase expresses a restrictive view of children and their role in the family and community as a whole. The thought was that children could be present during an adult conversation but not allowed to enter the conversation. Today we may refrain from quoting this phrase, but the words' essence lives on in many families and communities.

Due to technology, today's children are present in many adult discussions at an incredible rate in speed and numbers. Children see and hear unfiltered and uncensored video footage and conversations daily. According to the Administration for Children and Families, neglect is the most common mistreatment among children. Child neglect is the inability to provide the basic and necessary mental, physical, and emotional support that a child needs for healthy development. Many children experience enormous stress and anxiety. Children need to be listened to and given age-appropriate answers to their questions to sustain mental and emotional health.

In 2020, children witnessed various groups protesting in the streets on top of a global pandemic. The crowds said their names, Breona Taylor, Ahmaud Arbery, and George Floyd. Many children worldwide viewed and heard the detailed violent and unmerciful accounts repeatedly on television, videos, and other social media devices.

Like all children, Black children are impressionable. They see themselves through others' eyes. When people of color are viewed in society as a threat or as unimportant compared to other demographic groups, children risk internalizing these misperceptions about themselves. Studies show these negative and debilitating mindsets can question one's sense of value, personal worth and increases the probability of failure and fear.

Nazir's Big Question provides a basis for parents and caregivers to ask children, "How are things going for you today?" Presenting opportunities to talk sends a signal that it is okay for a child to say what's on their minds, giving them the freedom to discuss the issues that cause them anxiety and stress. *Nazir's Big Question* travels through the mind of a twelve-year-old African American boy who is witnessing history and experiencing anxiety and fear. What he sees on social media platforms frightens him. He has nightmares. Nazir needs a safe place to talk about his worries and thoughts with someone who won't laugh or think he's weak because he is afraid. Like most kids his age, Nazir wonders about life. He feels himself becoming a man but still very much a boy. Nazir's grandmother, Big Ma Nona, is where he finds one who is present, attuned, and attentive to him. She is a safe place where he is recognized and can genuinely be himself.

While the Bible does not answer all the questions we struggle with, it offers resolutions to many. Children need to know that God is holy, wise, and completely perfect. God is Creator whose righteousness and justice are the foundations of His throne. God loves us! Each of our lives matters significantly to Him, and our lives have definite meaning and purpose.

RESOURCES

Gunderson, E. (2020, June 8). Having "The Talk": How Families Prepare Black Children for Police Interactions.
https://news.wttw.com/2020/06/08/having-talk-how-families-prepare-black-children-poli ce-interctionsb

Helping Children Handle Stress - HealthyChildren.org (2020, December 29)
https://www.healthychildren.org/English/healthy-living/emotional-wellness/Pages/Helpi ng-Children-Handle-Stress.aspx

COVID-19 Resources: Child Evangelism Fellowship
https://www.cefonline.com/covid19/

The artwork was created using drawing and sketches and digital art Procreate.

For my family, Marc, my soulmate and safe place, my beautiful children Camillah, Joshua, Calah, and my daughter at heart Dani; and for every worker that labor and advocate on behalf of children.

Lightning Source UK Ltd.
Milton Keynes UK
UKHW051109170821
388950UK00002B/152